For everyone who has loved and does love me—B. B.

To Jojy, with love—V. C.

SIMON & SCHUSTER BOOKS FOR YOUNG READERS

An imprint of Simon & Schuster Children's Publishing Division

1230 Avenue of the Americas, New York, New York 10020

Text copyright © 2003 by Barbara Bottner
Illustrations copyright © 2003 by Victoria Chess

SIMON & SCHUSTER BOOKS FOR YOUNG READERS is a trademark of Simon & Schuster.
Book design by Mark Siegel
The text of this book is set in Cooper.
The illustrations are rendered in watercolor.
Manufactured in China
10 9 8 7 6 5 4 3 2 1
Library of Congress Cataloging-in-Publication Data
Bottner, Barbara. The Scaredy Cats / by Barbara Bottner ; illustrated by Victoria Chess.—
1st ed. p. cm. Summary: When the Scaredy Cat family's fears keep them doing things,
Baby Scaredy Cat suggests they might be missing good things as well. ISBN 0-689-83786-0
[1. Cats—Fiction. 2. Fear—Fiction.] I. Chess, Victoria, ill. II. Title. PZ7.B6586 Sc 2002
[E]-dc21
00-045059

THE Scaredy CATS

BY Barbara Bottner

PICTURES BY Victoria Chess

Simon & Schuster Books for Young Readers

New York   London   Toronto   Sydney   Singapore

Mr. and Mrs. Scaredy Cat woke up shivering.

"It's so cold!" said Mrs. Scaredy Cat. "But I am scared of closing the window. It may fall on my fingers. They will turn blue!"

"I see what you mean. You have to be careful," said Mr. Scaredy Cat. "All kinds of things can happen."

So Mr. and Mrs. Scaredy Cat shivered all morning long.

"Let us wake up Baby Scaredy Cat!" said Mrs. Scaredy Cat.

"*You* wake her," said Mr. Scaredy Cat. "If I wake her, she may be too surprised. I'm scared she will jump out of bed and knock me over!"

"I see what you mean," said Mrs. Scaredy Cat.

So they let Baby Scaredy Cat sleep, and they were scared and cold.

The sun came up and shone right into Baby Scaredy Cat's eyes, and she woke up.

"Let me find my new dress," she said. "It's so pretty and clean."

"But if you wear it," said Mrs. Scaredy Cat, "it might get a stain that will not come out."

So Baby Scaredy Cat stayed in her pajamas.

The Scaredy Cats went into the kitchen for breakfast.

"I would like eggs," said Mr. Scaredy Cat.

"But when I cook the eggs, the pan gets so hot—too hot," said Mrs. Scaredy Cat. "I'm scared I will burn myself."

"I understand," said Mr. Scaredy Cat. "You have to be careful. All kinds of things can happen."

"Perhaps we should go into town for breakfast," said Baby Scaredy Cat.

"That would be lovely," said Mrs. Scaredy Cat. "But then we have to go inside the car. And the car goes so *fast*. And when it goes very fast, I am scared. So I don't think that is such a good idea."

So the Scaredy Cats were scared and cold and hungry.

"I know!" said Baby Scaredy Cat. "We could play! You could bounce me into the air and catch me on my way down."

"Baby Scaredy Cat," said Mr. Scaredy Cat, "what if I throw you so high that I cannot catch you? I would worry and worry."

So the Scaredy Cats sat around without anything to do. Now they were scared and cold and hungry and bored.

There was a knock at the door.

"Who is it?" asked the Scaredy Cats.

"It is the postman," said the voice.

"What do you want?" asked Mr. Scaredy Cat.

"I have a package for the Scaredy Cats," he said.

The Scaredy Cats looked at each other. "This is *so* exciting," said Baby Scaredy Cat.

"Maybe it is a dress!" said Mrs. Scaredy Cat.

"Or candied apples!" said Mr. Scaredy Cat.

"Or toys!" said Baby Scaredy Cat.

"Please sign here," said the postman.

"But what if the package is packed with foam, and it flies all over the living room?" said Mrs. Scaredy Cat. "Then I will be mad."

"Or what if the package has shoes instead of candied apples," said Mr. Scaredy Cat. "Then *I* will be mad."

"And what if the package is full of toys that are broken?" said Mr. and Mrs. Scaredy Cat to Baby Scaredy Cat. "Then you will be mad too!"

Mr. and Mrs. Scaredy Cat told the postman to keep his package.

So now the Scaredy Cats were scared and cold and hungry and bored and mad.

Mr. Scaredy Cat opened a book.

"Will you please read to us?" asked Baby Scaredy Cat.

"But what if I do not like the story?" said Mrs. Scaredy Cat. "Or what if it goes on too long?"

"What if I get too tired to keep going?" said Mr. Scaredy Cat. "Better not to begin."

"I understand," said Mrs. Scaredy Cat. "You have to be careful. All kinds of things can happen."

So now the Scaredy Cats were scared and cold and
hungry and bored and mad and disappointed.

The telephone rang.

"Who could it be?" said Mrs. Scaredy Cat.

"Could it be Grandpa?" said Baby Scaredy Cat. "Or Grandma?"

"It could be," said Mr. Scaredy Cat. "But what if it is not? What if it is the landlord and he wants the rent?"

"He will yell at us," said Mrs. Scaredy Cat.

So they did not pick up the phone.

So now the Scaredy Cats
were scared and cold and
hungry and bored and mad
and disappointed and worried.

Since there was nothing to do, the Scaredy Cats sat together doing nothing until the sun began to go down.

"I love sunsets," said Baby Scaredy Cat. "Let's all go outside and watch!"

"But what if the sun is *too* bright?" said Mr. Scaredy Cat. "And it hurts my eyes?"

"And what if it takes too long and I fall asleep?" said Mrs. Scaredy Cat.

So, now the Scaredy Cats
were scared and cold and
hungry and bored and mad
and disappointed and worried
and left out.

"It is bedtime," said Mrs. Scaredy Cat. "Time to say good night."

"It may be bedtime," said Mr. Scaredy Cat, "but what if I can't fall asleep? Or what if I have a *bad* dream?"

"What if I stay up and worry?" said Baby Scaredy Cat. "I will worry that tomorrow I will be scared and cold and hungry and bored and mad and disappointed and worried and left out *and* tired—just like today."

"Oh, no! What can we do?" asked Mrs. Scaredy Cat and Mr. Scaredy Cat.

"Mama, Papa," said Baby Scaredy Cat, "I know we have to careful, but if all kinds of things can happen, can *good* things happen too?"

"Well . . . ," said Mr. Scaredy Cat.
"Well . . . ," said Mrs. Scaredy Cat.
"*Well?*" said Baby Scaredy Cat.
"Well, *maybe!*" said Mr. and Mrs. Scaredy Cat.

"Then tomorrow we could get the package from the postman, and I will untie the ribbons!" said Baby Scaredy Cat.

"Well, if *you* untie the ribbons, perhaps *I* could open it up," said Mr. Scaredy Cat.

"Well, if you open it up, I suppose *I* could see what's inside! Oh, Baby Scaredy Cat, what a clever baby you are!" And without thinking Mama Scaredy Cat yawned.

And a yawn is a hard thing to resist.

So, the Scaredy Cats fell asleep, and one by one, . . .

. . . each dreamed of being brave tomorrow.